LILA'S PASSION

ENCHANTED IN A HEARTBEAT

VESTA ROMERO

LILA

Jeez! Is this my destiny for a lifetime?

I groaned as I graded an assignment, crossing lines in red ink as my eyes scanned the paper quickly.

As I was grading the sheet, my heart sank when I saw the disastrous job this student had done, leading me to scrawl a giant **F** on it.

Although it's unlikely they would be pleased, my primary responsibility is to guide them towards the right path, not to cater to their desires.

My mind reflected on my foolish decision, made a few years back when I was still an optimistic person and felt like I had my whole life ahead of me. I'd always dreamed of being a teacher, but life had an altogether strange plan for me.

Instead of pursuing a teaching degree, I worked as a teacher's aide at a local elementary school. The pay was unimpressive, but the opportunity to work with children was a rewarding experience for me.

I was seated in my father's living room, where I often spent my weekends, staring blankly at the TV screen when my nose wasn't buried in the paperwork. At the young age of 29, I was already feeling the weight of my reality sinking in.

A single, soon to be referred to as a spinster, who lived alone, and was stuck in a dead-end job. If there was anything missing from the bleak picture, it was only a group of nine cats that would eventually feed off my dead body.

As I looked towards the future, all I could see was a desolate path, and a life of loneliness seemed to be my fate, so I resigned myself to it.

How incredibly annoying that men were never referred to that way. No, they were carefree bachelors, and no one blinked an eye when they remained that way for life. Women were doomed.

I was doomed. Doomed! Sure, I was being dramatic, but that's how I felt.

My father, a kind-hearted man in his seventies, worried about me all the time. He knew how hard and how dedicated I was to my job, but he also knew that I was unhappy.

With a look of concern, he watched me closely, and it was then that I realized I had been lost in thought, sighing continuously.

"Lila," he said, breaking the silence. "I know that

you're worried about your future, but you have so much to offer. You're kind, intelligent, and hard-working. You deserve to find happiness."

A sigh escaped me again, not sure what to say. His concern was appreciated, but I didn't know how to change my situation. I felt trapped, stuck in a cycle of work and nothingness.

"I just don't know how to meet someone," came my forlorn reply. "I don't go out much, and have no real hobbies or interests that would help me meet new people."

How pitiful I sounded even to my own ears. Is it just me or is it uncommon for someone my age to discuss dating with their father?

My father nodded, understanding my predicament. He had lost my mother many years ago, and knew what it was like to feel alone. After her passing, he had struggled for a long time. Having always been a family man, and without his wife by his side, he felt lost.

Despite the pain and sadness he felt, there was no giving up because he knew that my mother would have wanted him to keep living and find joy in life again.

So, he searched for ways to cope with his loneliness. He joined a support group for people who lost their partners and found comfort in talking with others who shared the same experience.

He also volunteered at a local charity, which helped him feel connected to life.

As a result, he could pick up new hobbies, and every week, he would proudly put on the ugliest shirt to play in a league. Darts! Prior to this moment, I was not aware that it was considered a competitive sport.

Every once in a while, he even had a proper date. Sad to say that my dad has a more active social life than I do.

"Maybe it's time to try something new," he advised. "Join a dance club or a group, take a gym class, or volunteer somewhere. You never know who you might meet. It worked for me," he added encouragingly.

I thought about his words for a moment. Maybe he was right. Maybe it was time to step out of my comfort zone and try something new. No idea what, but knew I couldn't continue on the path I was on.

Now, if only I had the time.

As I gathered the rest of my papers and stood up to leave, my father moved in close and hugged me tight.

"Just remember, Lila," he said. "Life is what you make of it. I'll always be here for you, no matter what, pumpkin." He knew I enjoyed hearing my childhood nickname, and it worked.

"Love you, daddy." I replied, returning the hug with a big smile pasted on my face. "Don't worry about me."

With his words ringing in my ears, I left my father's house feeling a tad better. Maybe my future wasn't so bleak after all.

Besides, doesn't life begin at thirty?

My spirit was lifted, but just for a little while. During my drive back to my place, my mind kept going back to the issues that were troubling me.

I'd been at the job for the past three years. Sometimes, it seemed like double or triple that number and it aged me. There was a maze I found myself in, and despite my efforts, I couldn't find the way out of it. Whenever something looked to be an exit, it turned into a dead end without fail.

Play with the shitty hand that life has dealt you.

This year had been the worst. I felt overwhelmed by it all as my responsibilities grew, but my pay remained the same. As the school year progressed, my workload became even more overwhelming.

The workload and stress levels of the teachers were so high that it unfortunately affected us, the aides, as well.

With so many students in need of extra help, I worked long hours almost every day just to keep up. Sometimes, I even struggled to stay awake during class.

My desk was piled high with paperwork, both at home and at work. The budget cuts were a common refrain that we kept hearing about.

Interestingly, some teachers I know have

switched to other careers, with most of them choosing to work in computer-related fields.

Sometimes, I wished I had opted for a nursing career like my friend Zuri. Her job at least paid more, even if it was just as hectic.

The next time we meet, it would be a great idea to have a conversation about nursing, even if I start as a nurse's aide. The pay would still be better than mine.

Quitting was not an option because I needed the job to make ends meet. Asking my father for help was out of the question.

As the school year drew to a close, exhaustion and burnout prevailed. I had given everything I had to the job, but it never seemed to be enough. However, a week ago, I received a surprise that made it all worth it.

One of my students, a shy little girl named Celia, came up to me with a handmade card. Inside was a heartfelt message thanking me for all of my hard work.

The card was filled with drawings and stickers, and it brought tears to my eyes. I realized then that my work had not gone unnoticed. I made a difference, no matter how small. It was an insignificant gesture, but it meant the world to me.

To prepare for the next school day when I got home, I took the time to iron my clothes and make sure they were wrinkle-free. Saving a few minutes during the morning rush can make all the difference.

Fuck! Fuck! Fuck! I repeated again and again after glancing at my underwear drawer. I had forgotten to take my laundry to my dad's. There was no clean underwear, not a single clean one for the next day.

Striding angrily to my laptop, I looked for the nearest laundromat, hoping that my use-in-a-pinch one was open late.

It was just a few minutes' walk, so I gathered up my dirty clothes from the hamper, stuffed them into a canvas sack, and hurried out the door, bringing along some more papers.

Might as well kill two birds with one stone.

2

SHANE

The laundromat was quieter than usual as I calmly loaded my clothes into the washing machine.

I'd lost track of time, engrossed in my book, before realizing it was almost closing time.

The place was deserted save for the old woman who seemed to be there every time I needed to do my laundry.

I had waved hello to her upon entering and hoped she wouldn't come over to chat. I wasn't in the mood for it and was glad I had brought the latest novel I was buried in.

Then, **she** walked in. I glanced up when I heard the door to the laundromat open, fully intending to return to my book, but that was impossible once I got a look at her.

She, with a slightly flustered expression, entered, clutching her laundry bag, detergent, and some coins.

I couldn't help but be drawn to her curvy figure and buxom charm. There was nothing subtle about her full bust, a narrower waist that flared into full hips and shapely legs.

Her auburn hair cascaded in gentle waves, catching the dim light in the laundromat. It added a warmth to her presence.

The comb that had attempted to hold it all in place sat comically in the middle of her head.

She was of medium height and I appreciated the way her dress hugged her figure as she moved.

What really caught my attention were her sparkling blue eyes and that bright smile, like a ray of sunshine breaking through the mundane laundromat ambiance.

The coldest of hearts would be melted by that smile and I would have given my eyeteeth to claim her as mine there and then, I thought as I shifted and crossed, then, uncrossed my legs.

Pretending not to stare, but still discreetly stealing glances as she approached the washer next to mine. I didn't want to seem too forward, but she was like a magnet, who pulled me in without even knowing it.

I found myself infatuated by her presence, and I secretly hoped she felt the same way.

She smiled at me, and my heart skipped a beat. I returned the smile, trying not to show how captivated I was. The laundromat seemed to fade away, and all that mattered was the two of us sitting side by side.

As we waited for our laundry to finish, we struck up a conversation that felt so natural.

She shared her excitement about making it in time before closing, and I laughed at her funny stories about laundry, and student stories.

I opened up about my day, embellishing just a tad. There's only so much one can do with a boring grocery store run. It felt like we had known each other for ages.

Time flew by, and I didn't want this encounter to end. There was a connection forming.

She was a bright spot on my otherwise ordinary day, a delightful surprise that made everything better.

I wondered why I'd never seen her at the laundromat before and made a promise to come at the same time every week hoping to run into her.

When the dryers signaled the end of our much too brief time together, I didn't want to say goodbye just yet.

I suggested exchanging contact information, and she agreed with a shy smile, which melted my heart.

As we left the laundromat that night, the intense desire to see her again consumed my thoughts.

The possibility of this unexpected encounter turning into something beautiful has me excited about the potential future it could bring.

I was looking forward to the unforgettable adventure.

3

LILA

The laundromat's glaring lights made me squint as I rushed through the entrance just in time before they closed.

My heart was pounding from the sprint, and I struggled to balance my overflowing laundry bag, detergent, and some loose change I had scrounged up.

As I scanned the room, hoping my favorite washer would still be available, my eyes landed on him.

The man, casually putting his clothes into one of the washing machines, stood tall with charcoal black hair that reminded me of a movie star. He seemed so at ease, completely unaware of his striking good looks.

Despite my flustered state, It was impossible not

to feel a subtle infatuation that not only made me wet but also caught me by surprise.

I moved closer without forethought because my legs decided for me. I feverishly hoped for an available washer next to his and I could feel his gaze on me.

Duh! The place is deserted. You have your choice of washers!

It made my cheeks flush because it was brazen, but his warm and friendly demeanor put me at ease. His eyes were like deep pools of rich, velvety chocolate that enticed me.

I saw a hint of playfulness and curiosity, as if he was ever ready for the next adventure that life offered, and I envied it. Life had already defeated me.

Beyond that, though, I detected a tenderness, plus they seemed to reflect his emotions, which admittedly stupefied me then.

Was that desire I saw in a fleeting moment? There's no way it could have been with me looking so disheveled.

Securing the washer next to his, I smiled shyly at him, feeling a sudden comfort in his presence.

He returned the smile, and in that moment, I knew I was lost forever. His eyes crinkled at the corners and his entire face lit up.

I felt like I was at the center of his universe and the world faded away.

Get a grip, woman!

As we sat side by side, waiting for our washers to do their job, we struck up a conversation that flowed with no dead air.

My initial awkwardness melted away, replaced by a genuine connection with this sexy stranger.

We laughed and shared stories, creating a bubble of warmth in the least likely of places, the cold, sterile laundromat setting.

When he laughed, his eyes danced with joy, and when thinking, they had a soulful gaze that left me imagining his dreams. I wanted to know the person beyond those eyes.

It felt like we were old friends reuniting after years apart. As the laundromat machines buzzed, I groaned inwardly.

Shane, whose name was previously unknown to me, would be seen for the first and last time. I panicked inwardly at the thought.

I was, therefore, elated when he asked for my phone number. He wanted to see me again!

As I had no prior experience in the art of flirting, I did not carry out any of the customary mating gestures, such as licking my lips or shoving my breasts in his direction. A mistake I regretted instantly. He just wanted to be friends, I assumed.

I still left that night with a sense of anticipation, wondering where the unexpected encounter would lead us. If nothing else, I might have made a new friend.

A new friend you'd like to fuck, admit it.

4

SHANE

*L*ater, after I'd returned home from the laundromat, I couldn't help but smile with amusement as I unpacked my laundry bag.

There, amidst my clothes, were some of Lila's belongings; a lacy bra and a frilly dress that certainly didn't belong to me.

We'd accidentally exchanged our laundry bags, and the realization filled me with both laughter and excitement.

The mix-up was a delightful twist of fate and I felt happy that it happened, not just because it gave me a reason to call Lila earlier than the typical three-day protocol, but also because it added an unexpected flare to our newly budding friendship.

As I held her lacy bra in my hand, I couldn't help but imagine her smiling face and those captivating hazel eyes.

The thought of reaching out to her brought a sense of anticipation, and I decided I didn't want to wait three days to make the call.

I wanted to hear that laughter again, to have another chance to share stories and get to know her better.

I picked up my phone then and dialed her number. As the phone rang, I felt nervous and excited all at once. The butterflies danced giddily in my belly.

When she answered, her voice was just as sexy and warm as I remembered from earlier, but there was also an undeniable hint of playfulness that made my heart race.

"Hey, Lila! It's Shane," I said, trying to sound casual despite the whir of emotions inside me.

"Shane. Oh my gosh, I can't believe it. The laundry mix-up, right?" she replied with a giggle.

"Yeah, that's right! I hope you don't mind a little extra cotton in your life," I teased, feeling at ease with her.

She chuckled and retorted, "Well, I must admit, your boxers added some excitement to my wardrobe. I might just wear them to work tomorrow!"

We both burst into laughter at the absurdity of the idea. Imagining Lila wearing my boxers to her workplace was nothing short of hilarious.

I quickly responded, "Oh, you'd be the talk of the school, that's for sure. But trust me, you wouldn't want to see me sporting your lacy underwear in the communal men's room. It would be a fashion disaster!"

Her laughter echoed through the phone, and in that moment, all my nerves and worries dissipated.

As the call ended, I smiled from ear to ear. The deep laughter we had shared was the best thing that had happened in a long time.

It was a connection that felt like finding a missing puzzle piece, and I couldn't wait to see her again in person.

We planned to meet up the following weekend since she was swamped with work, but over the following days, we spoke more frequently, our phone calls becoming a regular part of our routine.

Each conversation exposed new layers of our personalities, and I found myself drawn to her magnetic presence more.

She was smart, witty, and unapologetically herself, qualities that only added to her allure.

I couldn't wait for the opportunity to see her again. There was something about the accidental exchange of laundry that felt serendipitous, like the universe was playfully nudging us closer together.

After our chance encounter, I realized she had become a bright spot in my life, and for that, I was happy.

When the time finally came for us to meet, my heart skipped a beat as I saw her walking toward me.

She looked stunning, just like the first time. The

gorgeous hair flowed freely, her eyes shimmered, and that genuine smile was present.

While exchanging our belongings, we couldn't resist laughing once again at the mix-up. But beyond the laughter, there was a sense of connection and familiarity that made me realize this friendship was special.

Do you want to ruin it with fleeting sex?

I couldn't help but think there was more to our relationship than just being friends as we grew closer that night.

The butterflies that were fluttering in my stomach were no longer just a result of being nervous, but also the excitement that built up inside me about future possibilities.

*You're in love with your new friend. It **didn't** come as a surprise.*

5

LILA

Suppressing my excitement was a challenge when I saw Shane's name flash on my phone.

It had only been a short while since our laundry mix-up, and I had been debating whether to call him first.

Taking a deep breath, I answered the call. "Hey, Shane! What's up?" I greeted him, trying to sound relaxed, although my heart was racing and my heartbeat louder than the clock that hung on the wall.

"Lila! It's great to hear your voice again," he replied warmly. The intensity of the moment took over, and I swooned and fell onto the bed, my phone still pressed to my ear, reminiscent of my teenage years.

We both laughed about the accidental exchange of

laundry, and I playfully teased him about wearing my lacy underwear.

His response, assuring me he wouldn't dare sport them in the communal men's room, made me burst into laughter.

The ease with which we bantered back and forth made me feel incredibly comfortable.

It was like talking to an old friend, and I opened up about things I wouldn't usually share with someone so soon. Nothing was off the table.

"No, there was no-one special in my life." I'd answered when asked. I was glad he couldn't see me blush.

There had been none for a long time.

When he told me it was the same for him, I pumped my fist in the air. I might have a chance yet.

Shane had this knack for making me laugh. Even with the work I had ahead of me that night, I couldn't bring myself to hang up. His sense of humor and playful spirit were contagious.

I dared myself to wonder if there was something special brewing between us. Not only did I laugh, but the butterflies in my stomach churning turned into little exploding hearts.

Our laundry mix-up had brought an unexpected excitement into my dull life.

As I was reminiscing, I had a moment of realization that I thought like a teenager would.

Just like the time when my room was filled with

posters of my favorite singer, covering every inch of the walls.

We arranged to meet the following weekend. My first day of freedom since it was the end of the academic year.

I would have loved to do it sooner, but I had too many papers and other school duties that could not be neglected. The work didn't stop just because the school year did.

In the days that followed, our phone calls became a treasured routine. We peeled back layers of ourselves, creating a strong bond. Though I worried about over sharing, I trusted him not to hurt me.

That thought both thrilled and scared me, but I would embrace the uncertainty because one thing was clear; Shane had become an important presence in my life in such a short time, and I was excited to see where our laughter-filled journey would lead us.

Not in the friend zone, please?

6

SHANE

After what seemed like an eternity, it was the day for our meet, and I felt apprehensive as I headed back to the laundromat to meet Lila.

Seeing her again was all I could think about, and the idea of spending more time with her made my heart beat faster.

Despite my efforts to move forward, the possibility that she was just a coincidence and a fleeting attraction kept nagging at me.

What if the connection I believed we shared held no substance, just a brief instant, weighed heavily on my mind? These thoughts haunted me, but I tried hard to shake them off.

I didn't think so, though; it wasn't so on my part as evidenced by the plenty of stroking myself that I'd done over the past week as I thought of fucking her constantly.

My confidence in my ability to seduce women was unwavering. They seemed to be drawn to me, and I'd certainly enjoyed that attention. But something shifted when I met her; now, I no longer felt the same level of certainty.

I arrived a little early before the agreed-upon time. While searching through the crowd, I was approached by a woman for directions, and I appreciated the diversion.

Despite her flirtatious behavior, I refrained from flirting back as I would have before meeting Lila. It was fortunate that Lila appeared just then, and I could clear up any confusion.

Following our playful exchange, I suggested that we have lunch together at Tacarita, the Mexican restaurant nearby. It was a popular spot in Arelis Springs, and I knew the food there was delicious.

As we walked to the restaurant, I noticed the way Lila's eyes twinkled, matching my enthusiasm for the day ahead.

She was elated because she now had the summer to herself, her classes having ended the day before.

When she talked about the job, her eyes gave away her struggle, but I didn't press for more details. She would open up in due course.

Inside Tacarita, I greeted Lance, the bartender, with a warm smile. We were old friends, and I had occasionally filled in for him behind the counter during my college years.

Lance was happy to see me, and he welcomed Lila with the same friendly demeanor.

Over lunch, we savored the flavorful Mexican dishes, and I couldn't resist recommending the margaritas, which were very good there.

The tequila and lime juice blended perfectly, with just the right amount of salt on the rim. We both found them enjoyable while filling the air with cheerful banter.

Instead of my usual choice of beer, I went for the refreshing margaritas when I ate there.

Our lunch dragged on for three leisurely hours, with neither wanting to break the spell. There was something magical about spending time with Lila.

I shared stories about my work as a software engineer after realizing that somehow I'd neglected to tell her what I did for a living. She was attentive and truly interested in learning about my passion for software.

I told her about my project, an app that could help companies with inventory.

When the lunch finally ended, I didn't want the day to be over just yet. I mustered up the courage to ask her if she'd like to continue the day at my place, perhaps to share some coffee and more time together.

She hesitated only for a minute before saying yes. I settled the check quickly, and we made our way to my condo, me with a swagger in my step.

7

LILA

The day I had been looking forward to had finally arrived, and I couldn't help but feel butterflies in my stomach as I headed out the door.

To say I was excited to see him would have been an understatement. I'd thought about it all week. It had been an ordeal trying to figure out exactly what to wear to make a good impression.

I stood in front of my closet, but finding the right outfit was proving to be a challenge. I didn't want to appear too eager or desperate, but I also didn't want to come across as too demure.

Picking up dress after dress, trying them on one by one, with none of them feeling right.

The floral one was too sweet, and the black lacy one felt too formal. I wanted to strike the perfect balance, chic and approachable, casual yet sophisticated.

Checking out some fashion videos for inspiration occurred to me, but I buried it. I had nothing in my closet that would warrant that.

Then my eyes landed on a knee-length sundress with a pastel pattern.

The dress had a flattering A-line silhouette that stressed my curves without being too revealing. The airy fabric seemed perfect for the warm summer day.

With the dress chosen, I moved on to the shoes. I wanted something comfortable for our meet but still stylish.

After trying on a few pairs, I settled on a pair of low wedge sandals that added a touch of elegance without sacrificing comfort.

Next came the decision about my hair. I considered various hairstyles, from an elaborate updo to loose curls, but none of them felt right for the carefree vibe I wanted to convey.

In the end, I let my hair flow naturally, with just a few loose braids intertwined for a touch of bohemian charm. It was a look that reflected my carefree spirit and added a playful touch to my overall appearance.

Carefree spirit? Sure! Were you not the one who was recently unloading on your dad?

While looking at my reflection in the mirror, I noticed the bright red lipstick I'd applied earlier. The look was fantastic, but I didn't want my lips to be the center of attention.

I fully scrubbed off the red and opted for a light

coral shade instead. The color was subtle yet playful, a perfect match for the carefree vibe I was going for.

The completion of my outfit brought a sense of relief. I had struck the balance I was seeking; a chic, relaxed look that would hopefully make me feel comfortable in my skin while spending time with Shane.

Now, if you could only get your heart to the same point!

Shane was easy to spot as I arrived at the meeting place, since he was taller than most men. He was deep in conversation with a pretty brunette, their heads bent close together in conversation.

The sound of the girl's laughter felt like a stab in my heart, as if they were sharing some kind of secret. Doubt crept in, and I hesitated. A voice in my head whispered that maybe I'd misread his intentions, but I forced myself to crush it. I would see it through either way.

As I was about to reach them, Shane caught sight of me and his eyes widened in surprise, and the smile that had been on his lips seemed to freeze. The brunette turned to follow his gaze with a curious expression.

My heart rate increased and my nervousness grew more intense. With a shaky smile, I said hello. Shanes's look shifted from her to me and to me.

At least to my ears, the silence was deafening. I even wonder if there was one, but his eyes softened as he directed his full attention towards me, expressing genuine delight in his voice.

The woman looked back and forth at us, unsure of the situation, and I almost felt sorry for her. Almost. "Oh hey," she said in a sugary sweet southern accent.

Shane turned toward her and said: "Lila, this is Marcia. We were just having a casual chat. She is hopelessly lost, and I was trying to help her out with directions."

A mixture of relief and embarrassment washed over me at my misunderstanding and I chastised myself for jumping to conclusions. Shane's eyes were still focused on mine as he said; "Lila, I've been looking forward to this day since we arranged it."

I was on cloud nine with happiness, my heart almost bursting with joy. Marcia's departure went unnoticed by both of us.

I was thrilled because it seemed like the subtle details of my outfit and appearance had caught his attention, thank goodness, and, when he complemented me, I beamed from ear to ear.

When Shane suggested getting lunch together at Tacarita, I'd nodded in agreement. I'd heard great things about the restaurant, and was eager to try the food with him.

As we walked in, I noticed Shane's friendly demeanor with the bartender, Lance. They were old friends for sure, and the way they interacted only added to the warm atmosphere.

The food at Tacarita lived up to its reputation, and I enjoyed every flavorful bite of the beef fajitas with all the trimmings and chicken tacos we doused with spicy salsa.

Shane recommended the margaritas, and they turned out to be a perfect choice. The tangy blend of tequila and lime juice, with just the right amount of salt on the rim, was delicious.

Throughout our lunch at Tacarita, I noticed Shane's eyes lingering on me with admiration.

Shane told me about his work as a software engineer, and I found it fascinating. Learning about his career made me appreciate his intelligence and drive.

I knew very little about software, but definitely appreciated all the wonderful results of it, thanks to the work of people like him.

When the lunch came to its natural conclusion, I was sad. I couldn't remember the last time I had such a great time. Shane asked if I would like to have coffee at his place.

Duh. Music to my ears!

I agreed without hesitation. The prospect of spending more time with him was welcome, and I didn't find the request to be too forward. In fact, I had hoped for it in my inner thoughts.

I couldn't wait to see what the rest of the day would bring.

8

SHANE

As Lila entered my condo, it felt so right, as if she belonged there.

I was glad the cleaner had come by the day before, ensuring that my place was presentable for her visit.

I'd never been a slob, but having a woman over as of late was a rare occurrence, especially someone like Lila, who had captured my attention and affection.

As they say, you never get a second chance to make a first impression.

I led her to the kitchen, where we chatted as I made coffee. It was a simple task, but having her watch me felt intimate.

I wanted everything to be perfect and hoped the aroma of brewed coffee would add a cozy touch to the atmosphere.

With coffee mugs in hand, we settled into the

living room. It was a space I was proud of, my little haven in the bustling downtown area.

I'd purchased the condo after college, using the bonus I received from signing on with my company as a down payment.

It was my first enormous investment, and I had put a lot of effort into creating a space that felt like home. With the exploding real estate market, the value had sped up at a stunning pace that made my head spin.

Where would I go though if I sold? Everywhere was pricy, plus I liked it.

Sitting side by side on the couch, we watched an old western on TV. The show was just a background noise; my attention was on Lila.

I reached for the remote, intending to change the channel, but she playfully grabbed it before I could. Our fingers brushed, and the energy was electrifying and I felt chills all over my body.

Her eyes met mine, and in that moment, it was as if the world disappeared. There was an unspoken magnetic pull that drew us closer.

I could feel the mutual attraction, and my penis strained against my jeans, making me self conscious until I noticed the rise and fall of her breasts, which were rising quicker than my heartbeat.

The tension grew as we sat, and it felt like we were both on the edge of something powerful and exciting.

My eyes flicker as they travel from her legs, up those flared hips, and back up to her gorgeous mounds. Her nipples were taut and I couldn't resist pulling at them, and I was rewarded with a soft moan.

Without hesitation, I leaned in and kissed her, and she responded with equal fervor.

Our lips met, and time stood still as I felt the smear of her lipstick on my lips. Her eyes glazed and the taste of coffee lingered, adding to the sweetness of the moment.

The kiss was gentle, a dance of two souls finding each other in a sea of emotions. I wanted to remember everything, so I took my time exploring her mouth instead of diving my tongue in.

I realized that having her in my space, in my life, was the ultimate piece of a puzzle that had longed for completion.

We pulled away from the kiss with reluctance, our eyes locked, and a smile formed on both our faces.

Turning off the television, I got up and reached for her hand, which felt small in mine.

I pulled her up and lifted her to my eye level, continuing to kiss her as I headed towards the bedroom..

Her plump ass, like watermelons, was clasped in my grasp as she wrapped her legs around me. My cock thumped against her crotch.

9

LILA

When I stepped into Max's condo, I was filled with nervous anticipation.

It was the first time I would be alone with a man in a long time, and I couldn't help but feel a flutter of nerves.

The neatness of the condo spoke volumes about his attention to detail and the effort he had put into making it comfortable.

He prepared the coffee while I watched him move around with ease. I appreciated the warm, inviting space.

Sitting near him on the couch felt intimate and different from a regular bachelor pad meant for women. It was a proper home.

There was an old western playing on the TV that he switched on. I found myself more focused on him than the movie, even though it was one of my all-time favorites.

When he reached for the remote, I grabbed at it to keep the channel as it was, and our fingers brushed against each other, sending a shiver down my spine.

There was a moment where our eyes met, and I could tell that my feelings were shared. His intense gaze was gentle, and I felt drawn to him unexplainably.

When he leaned in for our first ever kiss, the rapid beat of my heart could be heard by him, I was sure.

The touch of his lips against mine was like a spark igniting a flame. It was a tender kiss that spoke volumes about the emotions we shared.

As I wrapped my arms around his neck, the taste of coffee and the smell of his cologne had me captivated in the moment. Nothing had ever felt so good.

As we pulled away from the kiss, a smile spread across my face. I buried myself in the crook of his neck for a minute and tasted the salty sweat of his skin between licks and labored breath.

I was ready for the thrilling sexual encounter ahead of me, and it filled me with excitement. It was going to be even better than I had imagined it would be during my daydreams all week.

It made me smile, happy that I was wearing my most seductive lingerie, which was damp with anticipation.

His hard member pressed against me, igniting a raging fire of passion within me.

I ached for his presence inside me, wanting nothing more than to feel him thrusting into me until I reached the brink of insanity.

His chest grazed my aroused nipples as if sending an electrical current throughout my body. It conveyed my desire, a transmission of energy between us.

I was more than ready, and I gasped with pleasure.

10

SHANE

As we stumbled into bed, I was reluctant to let go of those lush lips, but my preference was for them to be wrapped around my shaft while I ate her pussy.

But first, I wanted to see her in all her glory. I could feel myself tingly all over. I was nervous, impatient, and more.

The desire to bring us both pleasure was the foremost thing though.

I slowly undress her, taking in every damn inch of her velvety body.

My fingertips brush against the frilly fabric of her dress and I feel the rush of heat. Her lacy underwear is slick with pussy juice, and I smell it with pure delight.

Her breasts spilled out from her bra when I unclasped it. The succulent globes glistened in the dim light of the bedroom. I stroke them gently at first and admired their shapely curves.

Her breath quickened, and she arched her back. She was being driven mad with lust and stuffed a pillow in her mouth to stop herself from screaming.

"You're going to scream again and again," I promise her, before snaking one hand down to explore her hairy mound with its hidden clit.

I stroked my finger against her clitoris and felt her wetness as it trickled through my fingers as I spread her lips wide. Her breath quickened as my touch became more intense and she begged for more.

I alternated between rubbing the slick puffy lips and plunging my fingers deep, coating them in the wetness as she groaned louder.

I hear the wet noises of my fingers as I dove in repeatedly. Her skin was smooth and warm beneath my touch as I explored the folds of her femininity.

My fingers played within her moisture, teasing

and tantalizing until she was begging for more. I could smell the sweet, tangy smell of her pussy and the smell of her arousal is intoxicating.

My tongue darted back and forth until it zeroed in on its target, the giant swollen bud that quivered with pleasure.

Her hands were clamped around my head, my hair tangled in her grip, and her moans turned into whimpers as I sucked, licked, and blew into her delicious orifice.

When I, at long last, withdrew my fingers, her thighs opened wider, and I watched in wonder as the juice flowed freely. The wet and glistening pussy beckoned me to enter at will.

My body trembled with pleasure, and my hand traveled down my body to my cock, which I stroked, mixing my pre-cum with her love juice.

I then positioned myself over her and teased her for just a few seconds. I didn't want to shoot my load before she did.

Parting her matted hair once again to reveal those precious folds, I slide myself inside her tight, glove-like warmth with a guttural and satisfied moan.

With each thrust, I drove deep and our bodies moved in perfect rhythm. There was an indescribable rush of pleasure that coursed through me with each plunge.

She moaned with pleasure as her tunnel swallowed every inch of my thick cock.

"God, I love the feel of your heavy balls," she screamed in delight, having abandoned the pillow.

I stopped while fully impaled and rotated my hips so she could truly feel their weight.

"You like that?" I teased in a husky voice as we both listened to the squishy noise.

"Yes, yes," she screamed, her face contorted as she thrust her whole body up. "I've never had it so good. Never stop."

"I won't, and that's a promise." I assured her as I fucked her with powerful lunges until we both erupted. We reached the powerful peak together, and I flooded her grotto with my cum and her muff released me with a swish.

The rush of blood left me weak and my arms that had been supporting me could no longer do that. I collapsed on the bed next to her, satiated.

She rolled over on her side and crushed her soft breasts to my chest. My tongue darts over her lips so she could taste her own juices, and I pulled her even closer.

"This is the start of something beautiful," I whispered in her hair as I drifted off to sleep.

The giant grin on her face told me everything I needed to know.

11

LILA

Shane and I lay there, panting for breath, and I was entranced by the afterglow of our mutual satisfaction.

Our skin was still slick and sweaty. I rolled over to watch him as he nodded off.

My hands couldn't help seeking the outline of his body. I ran them over his strong powerful arms, the powerful biceps jutting out.

The intimacy we just shared was something I savored every second of, and I was in a state of euphoria.

Without shame, that was the best fuck I'd ever had because I'd felt the passion. That had been the difference. The two men who came before him faded away into the distance.

I listened to the soft snoring, and it lulled me into

sleep, my hand clasped in his like a child. It made me feel a part of him. It was a short but peaceful snooze.

Later, I woke up suddenly because I had the feeling that I was being watched.

I peered through heavy lids to find Shane looking down at me, his face resting on his elbows.

I smiled sheepishly, but did not cover my nakedness.

He embraced me then, and we stayed like that for a while, my hard nipples stabbing into his chest while my once again wet pussy rubbed against his protruding penis.

It was aided by my enthusiastic right hand that had closed around it and was now pumping up and down urgently, much to his delight.

"You seem to have found something you like." His voice teased.

"Oh yeah," I confessed, my hand already directing his dick to my wet entrance.

I had considered getting up to at least rinse my mouth, but that was off the table as he reached down to kiss me with such passion that soon had us going a second round. This time, it was slower, more intense, and more satisfying.

After our electrifying love making session, something shifted in my heart. He made me feel emotions I'd never thought possible.

Every touch, every kiss felt so tender and yet so passionate at the same time. I looked into his eyes as he looked into mine, and that's when I knew. I had fallen in love with him.

He became the only thing that mattered from that moment on. I wanted to spend every waking second with him, feel his skin against mine, and bask in the warmth of his embrace.

The desire to explore all the different facets of the relationship enticed me; It wasn't just sex, but also intimacy and companionship. I wanted to be part of his life, a major part.

It was as if he had opened up a whole new world to me, one that was filled with passion, pleasure, contentment, and desire. The list kept going.

Jeez! Can you think of more words to describe your feelings?

My heart thumped rapidly afterwards when he looked at me with such intensity, I blushed. Then he kissed me again, with more passion, and I swear, I felt his emotions come through that kiss.

Realizing that even though we'd only been together just twice, it didn't seem baffling, just fated. We were pieces of a puzzle fitting with no force or pressure. He embraced me tightly then, uttering those natural-to me-words;

"I love you."

"I love you too." I replied as I curled up in his arms, our bodies intertwined, and I drifted off to a long, uninterrupted sleep, grinning from ear to ear.

EPILOGUE

5 YEARS LATER

*W*ho'd have thunk it? Certainly not yours truly.

I was sitting at the window, looking out at the outside world from my perch. A lot has happened over the last five years.

In fairy tales, two souls meet and instantly know they are meant to be, but the idea of love at first sight was beyond my understanding.

Yet, here I am, five years later, living my real-life fairy tale with the man I met at the laundromat.

Shane, the love of my life and my husband. Husband, it still sounds strange to my ears, but oh, how it warms my heart.

Gone are the days of being a teacher, standing in front of a classroom.

My life took an unexpected turn, all thanks to my dear friend Zuri.

She helped me grow and change, so now I work as a certified nurse in the same hospital where she used to work.

The medical field suits me so much better, and I've found a passion that fuels me every day.

As for Shane, he's at present, the president of his own software engineering company, having ditched working for a company.

He used his brilliant mind and dedication to create an app that stops plagiarism and internet fraud, changing the digital landscape.

I may not fully understand the intricacies of his work, but I see the fire in his eyes when he talks about it. He's on track to be very successful, and I'm beaming with pride.

Our lives have intertwined with the big players in Arelis Springs, thanks to Zuri's connections.

I've had the privilege of meeting the enigmatic Billionaire Holden and his stunning wife, Kara, at a gala event.

Zuri, ever the middle woman, has facilitated these connections that have proven to be invaluable.

Shane and I have been daring to dream bigger than ever before by looking at properties in the Billionaire Haven of Arelis Springs.

My father remains a cornerstone in our lives, a constant presence we can always count on, a sage. He's settled into a new relationship and visits often, which is great to see.

It's about time; he'd been a widower for far too long. It seems just like yesterday that he urged me to find someone. Unknowingly, that happened the same night.

OUR WEDDING WAS as low key as it gets, exactly what I wanted. We went to the courthouse, just the two of us, exchanging vows that felt like promises for eternity.

In a joking manner, I had asked Shane if we could hold our wedding ceremony at the laundromat, to which he casually replied that he didn't mind. Just as long as he got to marry me, he said.

Although the suggestion had a certain appeal, I ultimately decided not to pursue it, and I think he was relieved by my choice.

It was simple and intimate, and it felt perfect, just

two short weeks after our first proper date. Though he was surprised, my father went along with it.

Afterwards, we had a small reception at Lulu's, the fancy restaurant that had catered Zuri's wedding. Our families gathered there, my father and his girl-friend, Shane's parents, Zuri, and her husband, Kent.

It was a moment of togetherness, a celebration of our love and the hopeful journey we would take together as a united couple.

The presence of our closest friends and family during our meal filled me with gratitude and caused me to dab at my eyes continuously, drawing laughs.

Although our lives had taken unexpected turns, we find ourselves in this beautiful moment that we wouldn't have experienced otherwise.

Then there's the matter of children. Shane and I had both been adamant about remaining child-free, but there are days when I waver as I watch Zuri kids frolicking with her friend, Molly's child.

While I admire the kids' energy and enthusiasm for life, the constant chaos would become exhausting for me at this point in my life.

At first glance, my friends' lives seem perfect, but the amount of effort required to raise kids makes me think twice. For now, we have things just the way we want them, full of love, adventure, and each other.

Although it seemed impossible, my father and his partner convinced us to join the dart league. Now, once a week, we wear those hideous shirts as a team. I'm almost liking them now. Almost.

I never thought I'd live this real life fairy tale, married to the man who captured my heart in an instant. Our love story may not be a fairy tale in the conventional sense, but it's uniquely ours.

I've discovered a happiness that surpasses my wildest dreams.

THANK YOU

Thank you so much for your purchase. I appreciate it very much.

MAKE MY DAY

If you enjoyed the book, you can leave a review on whatever platform you purchased it from, and **especially on my website**.

Reviews are crucial for indie authors like me who don't have powerhouse publishing companies behind them.

Just look for the WRITE A CUSTOMER REVIEW link. Your review will help with exposure to others who might enjoy the same.

Reading your kind reviews brightens my day and pushes me to be even better. Please be sure to let me know what you loved most about this book.

Join my newsletter to stay updated on new book releases and bonuses. Simply scan the QR code for the website.

Family legacy collides with fierce ambition, mafia romance style! Meet Ruth, the youngest of the notorious Moretti triplets, is hell-bent on shaking up the patriarchal norms that have kept her on a tight leash for most of her life.

Ruth's rebellion kicks into high gear when she flips the script, giving her father's choice of a husband a not-so-subtle hard pass and it's not the only curveball she's throwing.

She's got the hots for the mysterious Domingo, one of her father's most trusted men who's cooking up some secret schemes of his own involving dear old dad.

Buckle up because this family drama is about to take a crazy detour!

As Ruth stakes her claim to lead the pack, she's ready to face the consequences head-on.

Nothing's gonna throw her off course because she's determined to be the boss of the Moretti family, and with Domingo by her side.

Defiance had always defined her. Now, with passion and power added into the mix, they all come at a dangerous price: Her mother's life.

https://vestaromero.com/product/billionaire-mafia-triplets-ruth/

Mountain Man's Melody is a satisfying insta-love romance that unfolds amidst the unpredictable beauty of Gable's mountain retreat. Pilot Amelia, thrust into a storm, finds herself in the rugged seclusion that becomes the backdrop for an unforgettable love story.

In this swoon-worthy tale, Amelia and Gable's journey begins with sparks flying, where grumpy meets sunshine and laughter echoes through their intimate moments.

As they navigate the raging emotions, shared glances, and the warmth of a crackling fireplace, their love story blooms against all odds.

Join the fun as this steamy narrative breaks down the mountain man's defenses, revealing that the most enchanting melodies are discovered in the unlikeliest places.

Ready for a desire-filled read that unfolds when you least expect it? Mountain Man's Melody is your ticket to a love saga filled with passion and warmth that will keep you hooked from beginning to end.

https://vestaromero.com/product/mountain-mans-melody/

Can this billionaire stay in love with his angelic nurse after the bandages come off?

Zuri

I'm the textbook stereotype of an independent woman. A happy, dependable, and compassionate workaholic with a life my friends call boring, but who needs a man when l have a fulfilling job as an ER nurse?

I need to get rid of my sizeable loans first. Then, and only then, perhaps focus on love. All rational thoughts desert me upon meeting the mysterious blind man in my care and I make a reckless decision. Will it be worth it?

Kent

I'm a happily single bachelor who's just closed a huge merger and am on my way home when a terrible accident ushers me to the ER. I wake up confused and to complete darkness.

Temporary blindness they say, but are they lying? My guardian angel nurse has me weak at the knees at first touch and I'm in love, sight unseen. I must make her mine because she means more to me than my billions.

Is love truly as blind as they say and their love conquers all? or will the magic be as temporary as his blindness?

If you love the Cinnamon hero, Billionaire, and Curvy woman tropes, then this book is for you.

FIND ZURI AND KENT'S STORY

https://vestaromero.com/product/the-billionaires-blindness/

In a world of Hollywood glamour and glittering dreams,

one curvy scriptwriter's journey to love will make you swoon.

As she navigates the chaos of movie-making, little does she know that her heart's leading role is to be played by an unexpected, charming extra.

Sparks ignited on set as they fell into a whirlwind romance faster than any Hollywood plot twist she could have come up with.

But, when the truth behind her leading man's identity is revealed, she's left feeling like a pawn in a billion-dollar game.

Theirs is a rollercoaster ride through Tinseltown, where love transcends appearances and trust is reborn. Drama, passion, and redemption are plentiful as Serena, the heroine, and her billionaire producer find their way back to love beneath the Hollywood lights.

This hot and sizzling romance defies stereotypes, proving that love knows no bounds and that curvy is beautiful and oh-so-hot. You don't miss this spicy romance where chaos and chance conspire to create a Hollywood ending worth waiting for.

https://vestaromero.com/product/love-and-the-scriptwriter-ebook/

A curvy girl love story. Can these two polar opposites find love and make it work?

Cam:

It was supposed to be another dull day on the bunny slopes until this curvaceous and extremely sexy woman turns up just in time to turn my life upside down. Playing nurse has never felt so good.

Misty:

I'm a city girl at heart, a fish out of the water at this resort. I only agreed to come at the insistence of my best friend. Now, she can't make it and I'm stuck. All I want is the freebies that come with the suite. An impulsive decision to take a ski lesson with the hot instructor lands me on my bum and has me questioning everything I ever believed.

https://vestaromero.com/product/love-and-the-ski-instructor/

* * *

Will this rancher rope the woman in peril that he rescued?

Amber:

A year ago, having escaped my past and now living in this quaint town far, far away. Now, he's found me, and my new life is shattered. Finding myself in a dangerous situation, all seemed to be lost until my rancher came to the rescue. Now safely ensconced and guarded by him, I am finally starting to relax. Then, Axel, my bad-to-the-bone ex turns up again like a bad penny.

Fletch:

Happy to remain a bachelor, I am content with running my ranch. Then l meet Amber, a beautiful woman with a secret past. Rescuing and protecting her was a no-brainer, and not just because l crave her curvy body.

Can he save her in time once more?

If you love the age gap and woman in peril tropes, then you'll love Amber and Fletch in Protected by the Rancher.

There's NO cheating and NO cliffhangers. Sweet, sexy HEA guaranteed.

https://vestaromero.com/product/protected-by-the-rancher/

Can this grumpy billionaire and feisty pharmacist discover the love that neither one knew they wanted?

* * *

ABOUT THE AUTHOR

Vesta Romero writes love stories about curvy women and the men who love them.

She lives in Spain with her husband and Texas born dog. When not writing smutty books, she enjoys margaritas and action movies. She'd love to hear from her readers; reach her on Tik-Tok, Twitter or Instagram.

To stay updated on new releases and specials, join her newsletter via the website.

Vestaromero

Vesta's stories are short, sweet, and steamy with guaranteed HEA.

www.ingramcontent.com/pod-product-compliance
Lightning Source LLC
Chambersburg PA
CBHW061404160726
47995CB00001B/461